Mystery Tour

ALLAN AHLBERG · ANDRÉ AMSTUTZ

A Mulberry Paperback Book, New York

The Library of Congress has cataloged the
Greenwillow Books edition of *Mystery Tour* as follows:
Ahlberg, Allan.
Mystery tour by Allan Ahlberg
pictures by André Amstutz.
p. cm.
Summary. Three skeletons take a mystery tour
and uncover several mysteries by shining
a light on some suspicious objects.
ISBN 0-688-09957-2.
ISBN 0-688-09958-0 (lib. bdg.)
[1. Skeleton—Fiction.
2. Mystery and detective stories.]
I. Amstutz, André, ill. II. Title.
PZ7.A2688My 1991 [E]—dc20
90-2942 CIP AC

First Mulberry Edition, 1994.
ISBN 0-688-13640-9

In a dark dark town,
down a dark dark street,
in a dark dark car,
at a red red traffic light

. . . three skeletons are waiting.

"What shall we do tonight?"
says the big skeleton.
"Let's go on a mystery tour,"
the little skeleton says.
"Good idea!" says the big skeleton.
"What's a mystery tour?"
"I can't tell you,"
the little skeleton says.
"It's a mystery!"

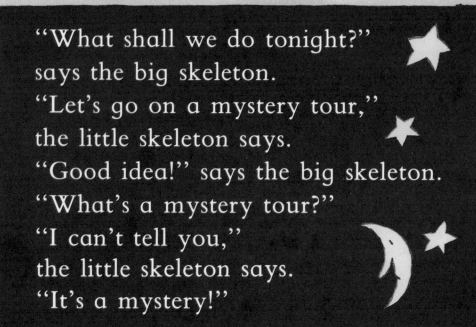

Then the red red traffic light
turns green
. . . and the mystery tour begins.

The dark dark car drives
down the dark dark street
to mystery number one.

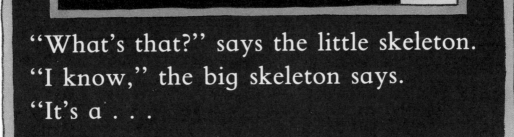

"What's that?" says the little skeleton.
"I know," the big skeleton says.
"It's a . . .

. . . baby in a crib!"

The dark dark car drives
down the dark dark street,
round the dark dark corner
to mystery number two.

"What's that?" says the big skeleton.
"I know," the little skeleton says.
"It's a . . .

. . . teddy in a tent!"

Two mysteries:
a teddy in a tent
and a baby in a crib.

The dark dark car drives
down the dark dark street,
past the dark dark park
and the dark dark zoo
to mystery number three.

"I know," says the big skeleton.
"It's a . . .

NUMBER
3

. . . black cat on a roof!"

And mystery number four.
"It's a bag of bones,"
the little skeleton says.
"No, it's not," says the big skeleton.
"If we put them all together, it's a . . .

. . . parrot!"

"Thanks very much!"

"Thanks very much!" says the parrot,
and she flies away.

The dark dark car drives
down the dark dark street,
up and down the dark dark hill
to mystery number five.

"Whoooooo!" goes mystery number five.
And what is it? . . .

Whoooooo!

NUMBER 5

Five mysteries:
a ghost on a train,
a bag of bones
(that was really a parrot),
a black cat on a roof,
a teddy in a tent
and a baby in a crib.

The dark dark car drives
down the dark dark street,
round the dark dark corner,
past the dark dark park
and the dark dark zoo,
up and down the dark dark hill,
in and out of the dark dark gas station
to mystery number six.

TO MYSTERY NUMBER 6

"I know what mystery number six is,"
says the little skeleton.
"Me, too!" the big skeleton says.
"It's . . .

Horror!

Gasp!

Howl!

Now the mystery tour is ended . . .
well, nearly.
There's just one more mystery.
"What's that?" says the little skeleton.
"Where's the car?"
the big skeleton says.

Where's the car?

A dark dark car
in a dark dark parking lot
is hard to find.

P

EXIT

The End